COVEN

OF

VAMPIRES

BY HANNAH PENFOLD

COVEN OF VAMPIRES

Editing by Leonora Bulbeck

Cover Design by Get Covers

Character Art by Ekaterina Vasilevna

Ebook ISBN #978-0-6455270-3-2

Paperback ISBN #978-0-6455270-4-9

Also by Hannah

Novels

The Crimson Scar

TSC - Coming 2023

Novellas

Coven of Vampires

HOB - Coming 2023

This book is dedicated to the Dimitri's of the world.
Your story is yet to be written in stone.

SENNASTONE

HANRAH

HOUSE OF RAVEN

CITY OF ALBA

CITY OF RUBIEN

THE SCRUFF

GOLD BAY

HOUSE OF GLASS

WHITLOCKE

CITY OF ORIA

TEALWATERS

ENVY

HOUSE OF CREATION

HAYLE

SAPPHIRE CITY

APPLEMORE

HOUSE OF BANE

PRISM ISLAND

MAYA

SCALE CITY

MOONHOLLOW

HOUSE OF SUN

HOUSE OF VELVET

SIAMOON

DIMITRI THUNDERS

1

As I scan the numerous shelves, my arms are filled with books that need returning to their correct places. I amble past row upon row of novels, tomes and publications that have been in this library since the rebuilding of the city many generations ago.

Reaching up, I rearrange a line of history books before adding the three missing from this section. One catches my eye enough that I put my armful of books down on the edge of a low shelf and start flicking through its delicate pages. They are stained with age, and the depictions upon them are starting to fade, but my lips tug up into a smile.

'Found a treasure have we, Dimitri?'

I turn to my cousin and fellow librarian, Bennett. We share the same dark brown hair, tanned skin and blue eyes. For as long as I can remember, we've been joined at the hip – so much so that we work together here in the Rubien City Library, our love for all things books and knowledge something we have in common.

'I think so. Check this out.'

Together we peer down at the chapters before us, images

of our city, which was once above the earth and in sunlight. 'Rubien before it was destroyed and moved underground.'

Bennett flicks through the pages, pausing on each picture to read the caption alongside it. 'To think that a city of innocents was annihilated by one hateful witch.' He shakes his head glumly. 'Now we all live in this cave. Who came up with such a strange idea?'

'Perhaps there was a particular reason the royal family moved their lives here,' I suggest.

A prince and princess of Hanrah – both only eighteen at the time – were the only survivors within the city's castle when the witch brought down her wrath on their people. No Rubien civilian is ignorant of the history behind our lands, of the drastic move all families endured from the sunny coastlines to the depths of this cavern, away from any other civilisation.

'A reason such as what, though?' Bennett mutters, running a hand through his hair. 'It still baffles me that they created this cave, that all within it was built by the hands of our ancestors.' He motions to our surroundings. 'It must have been a scary time for them all.'

I nod solemnly. *Scary indeed.*

'Anyway, I'm heading off now. I left the keys inside the desk drawer. Don't stay behind too late.' Bennett pats my head fondly as a farewell. He's done that ever since we were kids – he was once taller than me and happy to make me feel small, but now we are the same height. It still amuses me, though, so I never complain about it.

'Get home safe,' I say, watching him as he turns back briefly with a nod of acknowledgement. It wouldn't be the first time my cousin has been mugged. Like most people in our family, we are dameer – humans born with magical abilities. And like most people in our family, Bennett's magical abilities are defensive rather than offensive. He can see through anything – a teenage boy's dream, or so Bennett claims.

'Always do. Make sure you check the streets before you leave,' he says before heading out the exit.

From a young age, I have been able to see the future. As I've gotten older, I've learned to control the random visions and prevent them from occurring. I can also conjure images on demand – to see *what* I want *when* I want. As with anything in the future, though, nothing is set in stone. What lies ahead adjusts and evolves depending on a person's decisions.

I close my eyes, and my mind moves forward in time to see if Bennett will come to any trouble. The streets of Rubien seem calm and full of people. The shops and market stalls are open and bustling, as is usual for this time of day. Thankfully, I see nothing out of the ordinary. His arrival home is all I need to open my eyes once more to the books before me.

It's only when I go to put a volume back that a sudden chill washes over me, and the library's quietness becomes a cold silence. A shiver runs over my arms as I peer around, sensing something – or rather, someone – watching me. I glance between the books stored on the nearby shelves, towards the reception desk.

I find a woman standing there, waves of dark brown hair tumbling over her shoulders, contrasting with her milky skin. She wears a dress in an attempt to appear innocent, but I know better than to underestimate her. As I scan her face, she smiles at me, noting my observant gaze. Her lips pull back to show long, sharp fangs, her bright red eyes sparkling with delight.

'Hello, Dimitri.'

2

Her steps are silent as she walks through the foyer – the way she moves reminds me of a predator approaching its prey.

'Victoria,' I say, kissing her cheek as she embraces me.

'My love,' she says, her hands roaming over my arms affectionately. 'Are you ready to head out?'

I peer down at the book still in my grasp, its companions unsorted on the shelf beside me.

One of Victoria's brows rises – she's unimpressed. 'Where are the keys? I'll lock up while you deal with them.'

After I reveal Bennett's hiding place for the keys, she's a blur as she locks up the building, checking every door and window in the time I take to put away six books. In moments she's back at my side, keys dangling from a pale finger as she watches me put the last book in its rightful place.

'All right, now I'm ready,' I tell her, receiving a smug look.

Victoria takes a step closer to me, making my heart race at her proximity. I am still not used to her – the unnatural speed, her desire for me. It's as if I'm dreaming, and I'll one day wake up and realise this was all a figment of my imagination.

'I'm ready for something too …' She watches me from under her lashes.

'For what, exactly?' I ask. My voice is husky because, from the look she is giving me, I know *exactly* what she is ready for.

She doesn't answer but slowly pulls off my cloak and unbuttons my shirt, her lithe fingers cold against my skin as she unclothes me, and tosses my attire on the floor. My uneasy look towards the door makes her smile. 'It's all right. They are all locked, and all the "Closed" signs are up. No one will come in.'

'Good girl,' I murmur, making her cheeks flush with pleasure. My girl has always liked being praised.

Our lips crash together, our hands roaming over one another as she directs me blindly to a table. I sit on the edge, the perfect height to slide my hands up her body, my fingers tickling the skin under her dress.

'How was your day?' she asks, watching as my hand disappears under her frock. My fingers caress her breasts, making her lips tilt up in excitement.

'It's been eventful. The children came in today, and we had story time. We had a whole pile of book returns, and I had lunch at the Tea Shop,' I answer, knowing she doesn't really care but is trying to be polite.

Slowly I remove her clothing altogether and take a breast in my mouth, earning a groan. I move away slightly, looking up at her with an innocent expression. 'How was *your* day?' I mutter, grinning when her lips tilt down.

'Fine. You got me,' she concedes, crimson eyes upon me. 'I couldn't care less about what story you read today. Take me right here, on this very table.'

A zap of adrenaline shoots through me, and I scowl at her. Her vampire persuasion makes my body move of its own accord as I manoeuvre her body, getting it ready to do exactly as she has commanded.

She grimaces at her power over me. 'Sorry. Let me rephrase that. Please will you take me right here, on this table?'

'Say no more,' I reply, lifting her up. Her strong legs wrap around me, cocooning me in their embrace, unyielding and unwilling to let me go. Our lips find each other in seconds, like magnets that can't stay apart. My tongue slides inside her mouth, and she welcomes me, causing me to harden when she sucks and teases.

'I want you,' she murmurs, biting my lip tenderly.

Without hesitation I slide one hand gently up her thigh and taunt her with my closeness, testing how much she can handle, coming dangerously close to her wetness. She whimpers, wanting more, and I oblige. I trace a thumb along the very place she wants me most. I move it slowly in circles, loving the sounds that are coming from her lips, our tongues still entwined, and her nails dig in painfully as I increase the pace. Soon she is arching her back, pressing herself against me.

'Dimitri,' she utters.

'Yes, my love?'

She grabs my occupied hand and brings it between us, stopping our kissing momentarily. She puts each of my fingers down until only two are up. My brow quirks at her boldness.

'Right now,' she commands, her persuasion taking hold of me once more.

'Right away, princess.'

Her eye roll makes me laugh as I dip my fingers inside her and build momentum. Her breathing becomes ragged, and my trousers tighten with my need for her.

'You are so beautiful,' I say as she comes close to climaxing. 'My beautiful girl.'

One moment I am making Victoria scream, and the next I

am screaming along with her. Pain as hot as fire and quick as lightning strikes between my neck and shoulder, what feels like needles penetrating my skin.

Deeply embedded into my muscles are her deathly sharp fangs.

3

My lack of movement and paused breath makes her eyes open. Confusion seeps through her features before she realises her mistake.

'Victoria,' I murmur, voice barely audible. My body feels stiff. The adrenaline and desire are immediately extinguished as I stare down at her. This has happened time and time again, her desire getting the better of her, and I always suffer with the immense agony that comes along with it.

Slowly she removes her mouth, and I wince at the withdrawal, her needle-like teeth making me groan with discomfort – the pain is harrowing. As my blood beats through me, I watch Victoria fight for control of her bloodlust.

I move away because I need space, but her hands are upon me, and my eyes snap to her face. *She is a predator*, I remind myself. *Do not run, or she will chase you.*

In these moments, I am truly scared of her – fearful of the vampire that promises me I'm safe, when really we are both lying to ourselves. With Victoria, I am *never* truly safe.

'Dimitri,' she murmurs before I unsteadily move away.

It's my wobbly legs that make her move at superspeed to my side. She sets me down on a nearby chair and clothes herself as she frets over me. 'Sit. Let the dizziness fade,' she instructs, used to looking after me following her episodes. 'I'm so sorry.'

'You told me you could handle it,' I say, looking up into her inhumanly stunning face. Her eyes are apologetic. 'If you couldn't, you should have told me. I wouldn't have been so …' I wave a hand, the effort causing me to grimace. I can't finish my sentence, but she understands.

She kneels before me, edging herself in between my knees. 'It was so sudden. I didn't know what I was doing until you stopped. I thought I *was* handling it.' Tears brim around her eyes, and I find my hand hovering over her cheek, stroking lightly.

'That is no excuse, Victoria. When someone says no, it means *no*.'

She doesn't look at me but nods. We've had this conversation many times. I don't enjoy her biting me, and she knows that. But when I scold her for doing so, she makes me feel so guilty.

'I can't help it,' she whispers.

'You can.'

She meets my gaze then, my hardened eyes portraying how I feel. She claims to have no control when around me, but I know better. She wishes I wanted what she does. To become like her – a vampire.

'Did you know that younglings are most powerful in the first forty-eight hours? Even more powerful than mature vampires?' she says, hope lining her gorgeous features.

I sigh. I don't care about what I can and can't do as a vampire. I don't want the same fate as hers and never will.

'I promise it wouldn't hurt if you just relaxed. If you would let me—'

I shake my head, pushing her away from me.

She gets to her feet, a hurt expression on her face.

'I do not wish to be like you. I wish to be myself, in *this* body, with the life I already have.' It's been over a year now, and still she wants more from me – more of me than I'm willing to let her have. 'I don't want you to pressure me. My decision is mine and mine only.'

She takes me in from head to toe. Where I think an apologetic face will show is one of anger, of frustration. My heart races at the sight, her fangs gleaming menacingly.

'You have never accepted me for who I am. Never accepted my kind. You're just like the rest of them,' she seethes, tidying up her attire, making sure her hair is in place.

'Accepting you and accepting you turning me are two completely different things,' I say hotly, taking her actions as my cue to grab my shirt and cloak from the floor. 'Accepting *you* means having a life of love and adoration. Accepting your *lifestyle* means becoming something I'm not sure I'll ever be ready for.'

'"Something" being a monster?' she asks, quoting the term the civilians use for all vampires within Rubien city.

I know she's baiting me, wanting me to argue, but I don't have the strength to fight back. 'You are not a monster, Victoria. But you have to understand you are asking something life-altering of me. It means never seeing the sun or eating the foods I enjoy again. My family would live in fear of me.'

'We can protect your family. I won't let you hurt them.' She pauses from her pacing to look at me, to let me know she's genuine.

My mind wanders to my parents, their smiling faces as they hold my younger brother, Felix. He is only six, and if I turned into a vampire, like Victoria wishes, he'd be the first person I'd crave. A vampire desires the blood closest to their own – as my family, they share the very blood I'd want most in the world.

'That is not a risk I'm willing to take. And besides, I

would never be able to live in Alba,' I reply, my mind wandering to the dream I've held since childhood.

'You have been applying to become a librarian in the Library of Wonders for *five* years, Dimitri.'

'So?' I challenge.

'If they haven't accepted you already, they may never do so.'

My heart drops at her words. For years I have been requesting work at the most prestigious library in the kingdom of Hanrah. The capital, Alba, holds the largest and most renowned collection of tomes in the northern lands. Any who are accepted to work there are usually over the age of forty – the royals want their books to be safeguarded by those with worldly experience and the ability to educate. At twenty-seven years old, I have yet to be accepted, but this year I have high hopes – or rather, I *had* high hopes.

'Shove a dagger through my heart, why don't you?' I whisper, the hurt clear in my voice.

Victoria spins. Her pale face instantly morphs into regret. 'Dimitri, I didn't mean it. I'm feeling terrible, and I'm lashing out at you. Please.' She grabs my arm as I go to leave. Distance. I need distance from her. 'Please, let's talk this out. I don't want us parting on bad terms. Let's forgive and forget.'

Watching her reminds me of all the other times we've forgiven each other – or rather, the times I have forgiven Victoria, for forcing something upon me that I'm not willing to give her. Most times I would nod, let her talk out her feelings, contribute my own occasional comment, but this time I've had enough. This has happened too often, and I know deep down the situation will never change.

'Victoria.' She's instantly on alert, body stiffening as if sensing this isn't the usual fight-and-make-up situation. 'I can never give you what you truly want, and I will clearly never make you happy until you get that one thing.'

'No.' She shakes her head, hands on my arms, pulling me closer and with such force I can't fight it. 'No, don't say that.'

'You want me to become a vampire, like you,' I say more firmly, looking into her teary eyes. 'You want a partner who can be with you – understand you. I am *human*. I want to travel and see the world, feel the sun on my skin, experience new foods and cultures.'

'You don't love me any more.'

'I love you as much as I did the first day I met you.'

'Then why does this sound like a break-up?'

'I want you to understand. I do not want to be a vampire, and your pressuring of me will never help your cause. If anything, it deters me.'

'Because you don't want to spend your life with me,' she concludes.

'You know that's not true.'

She doesn't say anything.

I sigh, picking up her cloak and handing it over. 'This is for the best, Victoria.'

Reluctantly she nods and takes the cloak after a moment of consideration. She doesn't say a word as I escort her to the exit, open the door for her and watch her walk away from me.

4

It's early evening as I walk home. The stone streets of Rubien are unusually quiet for this part of my neighbourhood. Above me the stalactites hang precariously from the ceiling of the cave. My mind wanders to the sunny coastline somewhere above us, a city that used to be there, without stone walls.

Victoria will come to understand my decision. She will realise that once I've done my travelling, I'll be happy to settle down with her. We can find a home where she is safe and guarded from the sun – a place where I can be above the ground, away from the cold pockets of this cage-like cavern.

I continue to stroll towards the market, which is crowded. Shouts and the sound of smashing glass echoes through the air. I run towards the gathering of people, peering over their heads to watch the spectacle before them.

'Leave us alone!'

'Don't touch her!'

The yelling comes from a group of market stall owners. Their children and belongings are being roughly handled by two vampires who have decided to visit. Their bright red eyes keep the spectators at bay, and their fangs are sharp and intimidating as they hiss at onlookers.

One of them, with red lips and long dark hair, holds a young girl in her firm grip – at first glance I think it's Victoria, but I know she would never terrorise the people of Rubien.

The child withers under the female's hold, looking up with fright.

'I said I wanted some silks,' the vampire snaps, glaring at who I assume is the child's mother.

For years, the civilians of this city have been terrorised by these predators, their threats becoming more lethal as time has gone on.

The mother, whose hands are out as if to calm the vampire, has been crying – her concern for her child outweighs any loss to her business. 'Please, don't hurt her! Take what you want. Just don't hurt my girl.'

The vampire woman raises a brow as if pleased with the answer. She points a delicate finger towards a pile of silver material beside the silk she wants. 'Add in the velvet, or else I will snap her neck.'

'Don't you dare,' the mother seethes, her hands working quickly to gather the fabrics.

I'm unsure whether the woman is being persuaded or not, but she looks half terrified, half furious.

The mother's facial expression doesn't please the vampire. Her strong hands reach up to the child's throat in warning.

'Enough!' My legs move without my consent, my voice rising above the havoc. 'Leave the child alone, and leave these people be – you've scared them enough,' I say, winding through the throng of people until I'm standing next to the mother. My eyes are intent, warning glimmering in them. I've learned with Victoria that a human cannot afford to act weak in a vampire's presence. They only listen to strength and power – and as their inferior, I am naturally deemed puny in their eyes.

'Dimitri Thunders?' the vampire asks, to which I faintly nod.

I'm not sure how she knows my name, but I don't dare react. Glaring at her, I silently will the vampires to leave and never return.

Eventually, she nods, as if my request is a rather good idea. 'If you wish it, I shall go on my way.'

'I do wish it,' I state firmly, reaching for the young girl. The vampire lets go as I take the child's arm, and I hand her over to her mother, the woman's cry of relief making my heart race. 'Go back to where you came from.' I point to her companion, a female with short silver hair whose glare burns through me from across the street. Her arms are full of crockery, which I have no doubt she's about to steal. 'And take your friend with you once you've paid for your items.'

The pair share a glance before the silver-haired vampire lets go of the wares in her arms, and dishes crash onto the stone street. My jaw tenses in an attempt to keep myself from cursing at her. Everyone else seems to have the same idea – no one dares to insult her for ruining their products. Together we watch as the two finally walk away, looking back once before departing the market for good.

The mother alongside me grabs my arm. 'Thank you, young man. I can't thank you enough.'

'I'd say it's my pleasure, but I hope for all our sakes it doesn't happen again.'

The woman shakes her head, saddened eyes turning to where the vampires stalked off. 'I wish this were the last time, but they visit more often now, creating chaos and causing trouble wherever they go. It's the second time they've tried taking Anita.' She looks down at her daughter and kisses her head.

I've heard too many horror stories about missing children

in our city – the vampires deem them worthy of killing and feasting on when they are hungry.

'If only there were a way of getting rid of them,' I murmur, knowing full well this wasn't my first and won't be my last time standing against one of their kind. The newspaper always has an article to share when it comes to vampires.

'They are a plague on our city. It's a good thing we have people like you who are willing to stand up for the little people.' She squeezes my arm in thanks before tending to her ruined market stall. The neighbouring stall owners are gathering pieces of smashed glass along the street – obviously the sound I heard before.

People from the crowd start to disperse then – the bubble of helplessness they were in has popped. They begin to help those who went up against the vampire women – other stalls along the way are also wrecked – and more than anything, I want to go home and check on my own family.

5

I can smell baking as I let myself into my family home. My mother, a small woman with dark, glossy hair, mixes a bowl of what I assume is flour, eggs and other ingredients for cake. She looks engrossed as I quietly approach her, tongue poking out as she stirs.

'Mother.'

She jumps in surprise, the bowl in her grasp tipping over. I grab for it, grinning as I save her creation from splattering over the floor. She frowns before meeting my eyes, but her smile eventually grows as she seems to forgive my scaring her.

'I nearly had a heart attack,' she says by way of greeting, nudging me away as she puts her bowl down. She has a line of cake mix along her cheek, and I wipe it away with a finger and smear it on her apron.

'And I nearly lost the opportunity to have cake.'

She smiles broadly now. 'How was work, darling?'

'Really good. We got some new volumes in today that we need to find homes on the shelves for – and they're all the way from Siamoon,' I say excitedly.

'That's wonderful. Did you have the chance to read them

all before putting them out to the public?' my mother asks, cleaning away the discarded cups and saucers that are dirty and no longer needed.

'No, but I plan on heading into the library early tomorrow morning before my shift starts.'

She smiles at me like this is unusual behaviour. It's not. I spend most of my time at the library, books being one of my favourite companions. When I was a child, my mother would spur me on to make new friends, friends that weren't in the pages of books.

'And did you have a good evening with Victoria?' She gives me a warm smile as her eyes study me – no doubt making sure I'm in one piece. 'Although you are home earlier than I expected.'

Like everyone in the city, my mother is wary of vampires. She hates the coven that roams the streets and brings trouble to our homes, the destruction it brings upon our buildings, businesses and people.

I grimace, because the last thing I want to talk about is Victoria. 'We broke up.'

She pauses only a moment before she wraps her arms around me, embracing me as if I were a child again. I find myself leaning into her touch, needing a small dose of comfort. Slowly her hand strokes my back, so tender and gentle – just like her.

'My darling,' she coos as she leans away, starting to stroke my arms. 'You'll be all right. Things will work out in the end.'

'I broke up with her, actually,' I admit, making her dark brows furrow slightly, her blue eyes suspicious.

'Has she been pressuring you again?'

My lack of answer turns her face to stone. She is a soft lady – everyone loves her, and she is well known for her kindness. But when it comes to her two boys, she becomes a mother bear – protective, strong as iron and unwavering in the cause of our safety and happiness. 'She is a lovely girl, but love is all about compromise. If she cannot accept your decision to stay human, perhaps she is not the one for you. A decision like that is nothing to be taken lightly.'

'I know,' I murmur.

'Have some food with me. That will make you feel better.'

Together we prepare the table with lots of small plates, forgetting her cake mix. Two assortments of meat, slices of cheese and freshly baked bread rolls that are warm and smothered with butter. My groan of pleasure fills the room.

'Tasty,' I mumble, covering my mouth, which is full of food.

My mother beams with joy.

A racket sounds outside, and moments later my younger brother, Felix, falls through the door. Shopping supplies fill his small, gangly arms, but the bag tips and falls to the floor. Leeks and a bundle of apples tumble free.

'Felix!' My mother scowls, bending to pick up a stray apple. 'What did I say about—'

'Sweetheart, we're home!' my father yells before realising we are all right there. 'Ah, lovely. Looks divine, pet. Are there any leftovers for your doting husband and –' he peers at Felix, who is still picking up his runaway food – 'your clumsy second-born son?'

My father unloads the bags he holds and nods approvingly at my plate, half-eaten now as I stuff some bread into my mouth. My mother quickly makes up two more places at the table, and my brother takes a seat opposite me.

'What happened to you both? It's been hours. I was starting to get worried,' my mother says, stroking Felix's hair affectionately.

He looks up at her with a strange expression, and my father's grimace doesn't go unnoticed. Felix looks on edge, but his face softens slightly as he tucks into his food.

'The coven hit again. Stalls were turned over. We had fresh produce all over the streets …' His eyes flick to his youngest son. I get the feeling they experienced the same two visitors I came across. 'I think it's best we stay away as much as we can,' my father finishes, giving my mother a meaningful look.

She nods in understanding. 'It will never change,' she murmurs miserably.

'They need to be handled by the royal family,' I pipe up.

'They probably don't get informed of such things,' my mother answers with a huff. 'The coven controls all the communication towers and postal offices, and now it dictates what comes in and out of the city.'

My frown shows how little I really know of the vampires. When did they take over such vital parts of our home? With Victoria, I guess I've become ignorant to what really happens in the outside world. The pair of us existed inside our perfect little bubble, not wanting to pay attention to the war between our peoples.

'But enough talk of them,' my mother says.

A knock at the door startles us. A letter slides under the door, and we all stare at the envelope. It's royal blue in colour, the stamp of the royal crest upon its front – the peacock and her beautiful feathers on full show.

Felix is the one to retrieve it, his blue eyes widening as he takes in the envelope, and he hands it over to our father.

Hope lines my father's features, the same eyes my brother and I have peering up at me. 'For you,' he says, handing it over.

My brother runs around the table, his smile growing as he jumps onto my lap. 'Open it! Open it!' My arm wraps around him as I manoeuvre him into a more comfortable position on my leg, his small body coiling around me as I begin to open the envelope.

My mother's face contorts into an anticipated smile, her hand reaching for her husband's.

'You've got this, son,' my father mumbles, giving me an encouraging nod.

My fingers fumble and my hand shakes as I take out the piece of paper I've seen so many times before. The letter is from the Library of Wonders. All those I've received over the last five years have contained a rejection of my plea to join the librarians of Alba.

My eyes scan the paper as I open it out fully, and my breath hitches.

I did it.

Looking up at my family, I say, 'I did it.'

My brother howls in excitement, and I jump to my feet with elation.

'I did it!' I laugh, my brother wrapping himself around me as I spin us around.

My parents are quickly on their feet, embracing my brother and me, our family in a huddle together, and I can't remember the last time I felt this filled with happiness.

I've been accepted. I've finally made the cut. My one dream of going to the capital is about to come true. I will be one of the famous royal librarians, like I've always wanted.

'We need to celebrate!' my mother announces. She looks at the discarded baking and eyes the door. 'I'll buy some cake – strawberries and cream, your favourite.'

6

I'm being fuelled with shot after shot of Liquid Gold, an alcoholic drink that tastes delicious to anyone over eighteen and disgusting to anyone underage. The beverage warms me up, staining my mouth gold, as its name promises.

My whole family now knows of my achievement, and so here I am, drinking in celebration with my older cousins, continuing the night from our family-friendly dinner.

The group is dispersed throughout the tavern, which is especially popular with dameer – a spark of magic shines in the corner of my eye every now and then. Most of my female cousins dance with a throng of people, while most of my male cousins are at the bar, talking among themselves – the rest are in the restrooms, chucking up their guts.

I, however, sit with Bennett in a booth, watching as the night unfolds, the alcohol swirling inside my head. I'm drunk enough to be humming to myself, singing along to the music, but not drunk enough that I will forget the night.

'I can't believe you finally got accepted,' Bennett says, taking a swig of his drink. 'I knew you could do it. You're the most intelligent and capable person I know.'

His faith in me is not surprising. If I told him I wanted to fly one day, he'd be right next to me, encouraging me to make it happen.

'Thanks, Ben.' I peer around at my cousins, all having a great time, and my chest tightens at the sight. 'I'm going to miss you lot.'

'You deserve this out, Dimitri. You've worked your butt off for this opportunity. Don't get sad now – it's just the alcohol affecting you.'

'You're right, but I—'

My eyes begin to cloud over, and I know instantly I'm about to have a vision. Stuck in a trance, all I can do is wait for it to pass.

It's hot. My skin feels clammy and taut. I'm looking towards a large fire – so fierce it nearly burns my lungs being this close to it. Movement to my right warns me of company. Victoria doesn't seem to care about the fire but rather only has eyes for me. My heart swells seeing her, the beauty of her face, the desire in her eyes. She is talking to me, but I can't hear her. My heart races faster the longer we stand close, my teeth grinding in response to whatever she is telling me. Turning towards the fire once more, I can feel my hands closing into fists – something I do when I'm trying to keep my feelings under control.

Why am I angry? Or am I sad? What is Victoria saying?

My cousin shakes me, and I come back to reality. Bennett and his sister, Tillie, are staring at me.

'I think Dimitri is ready to go home now.' Tillie grins. Her dark hair is stuck to her sweaty face, and her shoes are off from all the dancing.

'I'm fine,' I insist, standing up to leave, but a wave of sickness washes over me. 'On second thought …'

'Come on. I've got you,' Bennett says, grabbing my arm and throwing it around his shoulders. 'Tillie, don't walk home alone. Make sure the others are with you.'

'I will.' Tillie nods in confirmation before turning to me. 'I hope you don't feel too terrible tomorrow morning. We all know how little you usually drink.'

'Thanks.'

My arm is wrapped around Bennett's shoulder as he leads me through hordes of drunks, heading for the exit. The moment we step outside, I feel slightly better. The faint ocean breeze from the cave entrance is flowing through the streets.

My cousin doesn't let me go as we walk across the busy road, the nightlife still roaring and awake around us. Some groups of young people practise their magic together, and swirls of colour rush through the air above our heads.

My mind wanders to my vision – will they be the cause of the large fire later on?

'What did you see?' Bennett asks, seeming to notice I'm lost in my thoughts. His steps are slow beside me, his body strong and steady as he keeps my arm around his shoulders.

I debate lying, but it's never been easy trying to bend the truth with him. 'A big fire. So big I thought I would melt if I stood too close.'

He quirks a brow, and I mirror him, equally confused.

'Yeah, I have no idea what it means either, but Victoria was there.'

'Maybe she started it,' he suggests, but I shake my head.

'No. I don't think so.'

We continue in silence for a while, and I realise Bennett looks completely sober.

'You haven't had many drinks. Do you want to go back? I can walk myself home,' I say, untangling myself from him, but he maintains his pace.

'I didn't drink much, because I wanted to make sure you had a good night and could get home safe without having to worry about walking alone.'

Seeing my goofy expression, he punches my arm. Before I can answer with something corny, a shiver runs up my spine.

It seems Bennett feels the same sensation, as his blue eyes widen slightly.

Did you feel that? he seems to ask.

I nod.

A flap of material snags my attention. In the distance, a tall figure with long silver hair, dressed in a midnight-black cloak, leans against a wall, his leg propped up as he plays with a small knife. My gut tells me this stranger is dangerous. My pounding heart tells me the same when he faces us, fangs bared in warning.

7

anic coils in my stomach and progresses through the rest of my body when I notice another vampire across the way, staring at us from a dark alley. The female's red eyes are observant as they roam over Bennett and me, scanning us from head to toe. A voice behind us jerks me out of my growing alarm as I clutch at Bennett, swinging him forcefully behind me.

'Which one of you is Dimitri Thunders?' the male asks, his red eyes curious.

This particular vampire wears a cloak of deep red with dark stains covering the front – I assume he's spilled something down it and conclude it's most likely blood.

My mouth doesn't move, my brain fogging with fear.

'Answer him!' the female shouts, her body suddenly up against mine. Her grasp on Bennett is strong as she rips him away from me. Her hands are around his neck too quickly for me to follow, her deft fingers ready to snap his spine if we don't obey. 'Silas asked a question,' she prompts, looking between the pair of us.

'Let go of him,' I demand, watching her hold my cousin as easily as if she were restraining a child and not a grown man. He tries but fails to ease her grip on him. 'It's me you want.'

Silas smiles menacingly. 'Excellent. We've been sent to fetch you, Mr Thunders – to make sure you get home in one piece.'

On any other occasion, I would keep quiet, but the alcohol in my system gives me courage. 'Thanks for the offer, but I'm doing just fine without you,' I say, motioning to my cousin, his face neutral but on guard.

The moment I reach for Bennett, the three vampires circle us, intimidating as they close in.

'We don't want any trouble,' I murmur, my eyes stuck on Bennett. I try to convey that the moment the woman loosens her grip, he is to run, but he doesn't look at me. Rather, he looks at the vampire closest to me.

'Come with us,' the one with long silver hair says, his teeth so sharp they could tear me apart without much effort.

'Only if you leave him alone,' I say, watching as the female's face slides into a sly smile. 'Unharmed,' I add, and her eyes harden with what looks to be dismay.

The three of them share a glance as if debating whether to punish me for speaking up against them. The female vampire pouts, stroking a thumb down Bennett's cheek, and his eyes widen with fear. The sight torments me.

'What do you say, Lazarus?' she says to the silver-haired vampire.

He debates the options silently for a moment before nodding once in answer.

I get the sense they are talking about something different.

'Very well.' She smirks.

My hair is yanked by the female, her long and sharp nails scraping along my scalp. For a wild moment, I'm ecstatic Bennett is finally free – until Lazarus takes hold of him instead.

My stomach blooms with pain as the woman punches me

in the gut before kicking me in my knees. The hard stone street makes my legs bark in pain. She chuckles, watching me roll onto my back, my eyes wide as I study her. She is erratic, and I hate that – her unpredictability scares me.

'Thana,' Silas warns, as if telling her to finish her business and be quick about it.

She leans over me with a wide grin that makes my body stiffen. 'You never specified that *you* should be left unharmed.'

I refrain from answering, and she finds delight in my reaction.

'Go on. Say what you want to say, human.'

'Demon,' I whisper, knowing she can hear me.

She laughs, amusement gleaming in her red gaze. 'You smell too good to tempt me like that,' she says, licking her lips.

I move away, instinctively putting my hands up as a barrier between us. It's the wrong move. A predator and her prey. She senses me wanting to escape, and the beast inside her can't help but want to chase me.

She jumps for me, sharp teeth biting into my neck, and she sucks up big mouthfuls without my consent. A scream escapes my lips, my arms and legs thrashing, trying to get her off me, but the more she takes, the more I can feel my limbs weaken, my strength leaving me.

Bennett roars as he runs for me, having been thrown away by Lazarus. My cousin looks mad, his eyes glowing with fury as he tries to fight for freedom, to save me from the female's grasp, but he is stopped by Lazarus, who snaps his neck as if it were a twig.

My cries of horror and sorrow go unheard.

'Enough, Thana!' Silas barks, ripping the female away from me finally.

My shoulder aches and burns from her attack. The

feeling of needles penetrating my skin makes me shudder – a feeling I wish never to feel again.

'Sorry,' she utters with no remorse, wiping her mouth with her sleeve.

My gaze stays glued to Bennett's body, his lifeless eyes staring up at the ceiling of the cave. My hand edges towards him to see if he is all right, but I know deep down he's gone.

'What have you done?' I whisper, my words shaky.

Lazarus steps on my hand, preventing me from touching my cousin.

My eyes turn upwards to see his amusement. 'Bastard.'

'He won't be pleased with either of you.' Silas frowns, looking at my wounded neck with an annoyed expression. He urges his male companion to remove his foot from my now-aching hand. 'He is damaged goods. You'd better pray he is in a good mood tonight.'

Silas – the only one who seems to have control of himself – roughly yanks me to my feet, but my legs feel unsteady and buckle beneath me. He takes it upon himself to throw me over his shoulder like a rag doll, his bones digging into my stomach painfully.

'Clean up this mess,' Silas orders his companions as he turns away.

My cousin is being left with the two of them.

'No! Put me down! Put me down! I can't leave him!' I kick my legs, but Silas's grip on them is like steel – immovable.

'Shut up, human. The lord of vampires will not take kindly to your behaviour,' he answers, whisking me away at superspeed.

8

I'm close to vomiting by the time I'm dropped onto the floor, my breathing haggard and my eyes still trying to focus, the blur of the streets messing with my head.

We are in a large chamber that is strangely airy but reeks of blood. My nose wrinkles at the smell. I've been brought to a long, narrow room with an extensive table that can seat at least ten people. With a yank on my arm, Silas hauls me to my feet. My gaze falls upon a dangerous-looking vampire at the head of the table.

I stumble as I'm pushed roughly towards him. A strong hand shoves my head down upon the stone, pressing my cheek against the hard surface, while another holds my hands behind my back. The stranger, with his blood-red eyes, observes me with amusement. He has a goblet of crimson liquid, and I somehow know it's fresh.

'As requested, Lord Atticus,' Silas says in greeting, his fingers digging into my scalp and wrists.

Lord Atticus hums unfavourably. 'I didn't know this was Victoria's … taste in men.' He sneers down at me but doesn't seem fazed by my reddening face. The hand pressing my face against the table is making my head start to throb. 'My daughter never asks for anything, however, so this is surprising.'

'Shall we chain him, my lord?' Lazarus asks, coming into my field of vision. Not too far behind him is Thana, watching me intently.

The lord of vampires studies me, as if considering whether he wants his prisoner to be caged or not. 'Yes. I think we should dine together. What do you say?' He peers up at his companions, and they share a smile.

My stomach drops. I know this can't be good.

'Victoria has spoken much about you,' Lord Atticus claims, making me frown.

'Victoria?' I repeat, wondering if my aching head is understanding him correctly. 'As in *my* Victoria?'

'He's not very bright, is he?' the lord says to his minions.

My nose wrinkles. Victoria never spoke of her family – she became touchy every time I mentioned my own. But when I first asked about relatives, she denied having any – yet here I am in the presence of Lord Atticus, the leader of the vampires, who claims to be her father.

'She never mentioned you,' I state, annoyance spreading through me.

'Strange. We have such a close bond,' the lord answers, making me think quite the opposite. 'Regardless, she wishes you to turn. So consider tonight an initiation present from us.'

Now I realise why they wanted me specifically.

Fear hits me hard in the chest. My vision blurs, and my head spins frantically. I think I'm going to pass out. 'No. Please, don't do this,' I beg, my head hurting more as I jerk against Silas's hold on me. My bound hands squirm against his iron grip.

'Oh?' The lord feigns curiosity.

'I'll do anything. Please don't turn me.'

The vampire's gaze doesn't waver as he stands. He

clutches my arm and yanks me out of Silas's grasp. I hiss at the pain as my arm is nearly torn from its socket.

'Are you telling me you do not wish to be with Victoria forever?' Lord Atticus asks me, making me lean away instinctively.

'I want to be with Victoria, but not like this.'

'Your miserable human life will end shortly. That will not do. Victoria deserves forever.'

'I agree. She does deserve that,' I answer honestly, but I don't realise what I've implied until the words are out of my mouth. The vampires' smiles are devilish, and I flounder under Lord Atticus's hold.

'Then it is settled.' The lord releases me briefly.

Lazarus has me in his clutches in seconds, giving me no chance to bolt.

Chains from beneath the table are brought above, four of them, made of obsidian metal. The black-coloured restraints contain magical properties to stop a dameer, like myself, from using their powers – not that my abilities could defend me in a situation like this.

Slowly the vampires begin to clamp my ankles and wrists in the restraints, the vampires' eyes widening with anticipation. I flail and buck, hoping to deter them, but their hands are stronger than anything I've felt before. They are unmoving and unapologetic as they seal my fate – my body is sprawled upon the table like their own personal feast.

'You'll not regret the decision. You'll be powerful like us,' Thana says, as if that's what it really means to be a vampire – to have power over others.

'No, don't do it. I don't want this!' I cry, trying but failing against the chains that hold me.

Silas approaches my left, his fangs so long I blanch. Thana takes my right side, and she eyes my arm up like a prize, her desire for my blood no doubt tenfold now she's had a taste of me already. Lazarus steps back and lets the lord of vampires have my neck, while he watches and waits for his turn.

Lord Atticus doesn't mention the puncture marks already in my shoulder, but his glance towards Thana is enough to know she'll be dealt with accordingly. Instead, he moves to my other shoulder, a fresh side for him to work with.

'A little advice, Dimitri,' Lord Atticus murmurs, his voice soft and silken against my ear. 'Don't resist, or this will *really* hurt.' He laughs, making my heart stutter.

I am just a mouse caught in a very dangerous trap to these creatures.

'Please, it doesn't have to be this way,' I plead, feeling tears stream from my eyes. Panic consumes me – my future is fading away the closer the vampire inches towards my throat. I can't help but stare at his open mouth, the long, sharp fangs right *there* – taunting me.

'It's always the ones that don't want to be changed that end up enjoying it the most,' Lord Atticus declares as his fingers slide through my hair. He quickly yanks my head to the side, my neck a gift for him, and he clamps down without hesitation.

I scream. Teeth as sharp as needles pierce into my skin on all sides, Thana and Silas also taking their fair share of blood from me. My arms begin to feel heavy, lacking in strength. My neck feels sore, and a burning spreads through my shoulder, down my back and across my chest.

The trio suck up large mouthfuls of my blood, draining me slowly, and I start to feel my head spin. My mind reels with the agony rushing through my limbs, with the thought my blood is being drained from me – like a pig in a butcher's shop.

'How does he taste?' Lazarus asks with amusement as Lord Atticus lifts his head for a breath.

'Like Liquid Gold. But strangely, I don't mind it.' He

smiles before dipping his head for more of what I have to offer.

My fighting body soon gives up, the life withdrawing from me as I lie upon the table, the lanterns above me blazing as my eyes begin to flutter. I feel weightless but with an incredible layer of pain throughout my shoulder and arms. My body hates every moment, wanting to expel the feeling of sharp fangs penetrating my skin and taking whatever they can get.

'The less you fight, the more pleasurable it will be for you,' Thana reminds me, but I'm not listening. I don't give a fuck if it will feel good. I don't *want* this.

'I'm begging you. Stop. Please,' I whimper, and the group laughs.

'You'll thank us soon enough.' Lazarus smiles.

9

I wake up in a room painted in gold and maroon. The bed I lie upon is soft and cushioned, and the room itself is cluttered with dark stone furniture. Finding a looking glass on the nearby dressing table, I grasp for it. The first thing I see is the change to my eyes. Crimson. Ruby red. The colour of blood.

'Holy Hanrah, no,' I whisper in horror. My hands reach up as I gape at my reflection, my mouth opening in disgust. Fangs – shiny and new – peep out from beneath my lips. I rear back as my tongue trails over them. Real – too fucking real. 'No, no, no, no.'

This is a horrible dream. A terrible nightmare that I will wake up from soon. Sounds from outside make me jump to my feet. Their voices are loud even through the walls, their words as clear as if they were standing next to me.

'See how the youngling is. He should be awake soon, and he will be very hungry, I suspect.'

I panic silently. I need to leave. I can't be associated with these demons. I need to go home.

Home.

What will my family say about me now? Will they think I

wanted this? No. They knew this wasn't what I yearned for. I had so many plans and now … ruined. Destroyed.

Grief racks my chest, my sobs quiet as I think of my dream to work in the Library of Wonders – now lost, my efforts all for nothing. Thrown away because of these … monsters. Yes, monsters. Victoria is a *monster*. Her father, the lord, is a *monster*.

I'll make them pay, I promise myself, hatred filling every part of me. My thoughts go to the hundreds of ways I could hurt them, how I can make them suffer as I have.

I clamber towards the curtain-covered window across the room. I heave the window open with such ease that I'm surprised for a moment before remembering my new vampire strength. I leap down from the second storey without a hint of pain and run.

As I travel through the city, I note how all the humans and dameer live on like nothing has happened, as if my life hasn't been tipped over and rearranged so violently. I envy them – hate them, even – that they have their own, normal lives to attend to while I … I don't know what to do now.

Revenge.

The word clangs inside my brain, reverberating around my skull, spelling itself out over and over for me to see.

Revenge. Revenge. Revenge. Revenge.

I will take revenge on those who have wronged me. I will make them pay for what they have done to me, what they have done to countless others. I will make them pay for everything I have lost because of one person's decision – a decision that has ruined my life forever.

A memory pops into my head – Victoria as she feeds me more facts about vampirism after biting me, hoping to soothe me with stupid details about how being like her will make everything better.

'Did you know that younglings are most powerful in the first forty-eight hours? Even more powerful than mature vampires?'

I pause, hiding within an alley between a pet shop and a tailor's. Peering down at my pale hands, I can feel the strength course through me, my energy unlimited.

More powerful.

Forty-eight hours to complete my plan. Forty-eight hours to set things right in this city.

I head towards home, to where my family is, and with my new-found speed, it takes no time to approach my front door. Quietly I open the entrance. At this time of the morning, my mother is having a cup of tea while reading her book. She looks up, and the scent of her fear hits me as her face scrunches up, a scream about to erupt from her lips. As quick as an adder, I'm upon her, my hand gentle as I cover her mouth.

'Don't scream. I won't hurt you.'

She reacts strangely, her back straightening, her lips pressing together as if I've glued them shut. I reel back in shock. *Persuasion.* I just used persuasion on my own mother.

'It's all right, Ma. It's me,' I say, trying not to think too deeply about what I have just done.

Understanding forms in her expression. She studies my face, terror – not *of* me but *for* me – spreading over her features in waves.

'Dimitri,' she utters, her hands shaky as she reaches for my cheek. 'What's happened to you?'

'I don't have much time,' I rush, kneeling beside her, becoming smaller so as not to frighten her. 'I was turned against my will. I only have so much time before the blood-lust starts to creep in. But you'll be in danger the moment it hits. You need to get Pa and Felix out of this cave. You need to get the next boat out of Rubien and go somewhere in the full blaze of the sun, where I can't follow you.'

My mother's mouth widens in panic, but I shake my head, not letting her interrupt me.

'You need to leave as soon as I'm out the door. You have

to understand, I don't *want* to hurt you, but I don't know how much control I'll have. I'm not *me* any more, Ma. I'm something entirely different, and I'm *scared*.'

'Dimitri, we can figure something out,' she offers, but I take her hands in mine.

'Look at me. My eyes are crimson. I am without a soul now. It's been ripped away from me, and if you don't leave, *you* will get hurt. *Felix* will be hurt.' I know the mention of my brother will make her realise the gravity of the situation. 'He will not be able to run, nor will you or Pa be able to fight me off. I will *win*, and I will *hate* myself for it.'

Tears trickle down her face, and I squeeze her fingers as tenderly as I can.

'Promise me you'll leave. I need your word,' I urge.

She reluctantly nods. 'I promise, my sweet boy. I promise I'll get us all out of the city.'

'You can write to me, but I must never know where you are.'

She purses her lips but doesn't disagree.

'I love you, Ma. Tell Pa and Felix I love them too, with every fibre of my being. Never *ever* forget that. I dreamed of a better future for us all, but you must live it without me now – for Felix's sake.'

'Dimitri, I—' She breaks down into sobs, and I hold her close.

'I'm going to miss you so much,' I whisper, making her cry even louder. 'I have to go.'

Her arms wrap around me then, and my instincts tell me she is human. She is breakable and is potential *food*. I can tell she senses my change of demeanour.

'The change is coming,' she says with a sniffle.

I nod, getting to my feet quickly. I approach the door and swing it open, looking back one more time. 'Go get them right now. You don't have much time left, and when it does run out, I'll be the most hated vampire in the whole of Hanrah, and you'll all be targets too.'

My mother wrings her hands with nerves. 'What are you going to do?'

A flicker of hope fills my chest. I will do what it takes to keep my family safe. I will do what is needed to make my city safe once more. I will devote my new immortal life to saving those who can't defend themselves from creatures who have no morals and understand no distinction between right and wrong. I will take revenge for Bennett, my cousin and best friend, who was killed for being brave, killed while fighting for *me*.

My hands turn into fists, loathing coating every emotion inside me. 'I'm going to destroy the coven from the bottom up. Rubien will be free of vampires for evermore.'

VICTORIA MILLER

IO

Victoria

Shouts and screams erupt through the streets, and I'm alerted to a mass of running civilians. For once they don't care about my presence – they have found a greater danger in their midst.

Curious, I stalk towards the chaos, people shoving me, pushing me out of their way to get away from whatever has caused so much fear. The blood pumping through their fragile bodies makes me hungry, but not hungry enough to forget my curiosity.

It's a great surprise when I come across a large fire with one lonely figure standing before it, watching it burn and crackle as it grows more vigorous.

'How did you find enough kindling to light such a blaze?' I ask the stranger as I approach. He turns, and my throat tightens, my heart racing inside my chest. 'Dimitri?'

My hands reach out of their own accord, needing to touch him, needing to see if this is real. His blood-red eyes study me intently, his fanged mouth relaxed as he watches me process his new body. But what scares me is the blood splattered all over his clothes and skin. His face is covered in droplets of rust-coloured liquid.

'Are you hurt?' I ask, earning a shake of his head. He doesn't seem to want to talk about the blood on him, so I let the topic go for now. 'You look …'

He peers into my eyes, his once ocean-blue gaze now ruby red, waiting for the rest of my sentence.

'Beautiful,' I can't help but whisper as I take him in. He looks leaner and much sharper than before – his human features were no doubt cut away by the brutality of his turning.

He steps closer to me, inhaling deeply as his fisted hands uncoil slightly. The fire before us somehow becomes hotter, and I can't help but ache for him.

Together. We can finally be together.

Nerves bubble up inside me as I wonder how he is feeling at this moment. When he was human, I could smell the emotions he experienced – could feel the heat rise in his cheeks when he felt embarrassed. But now his skin is colour-less. His lips don't move, and his eyes are deep wells full of *nothing*.

'Are you all right?' I find him watching me carefully when I meet his gaze. 'Do you feel stronger?'

He nods, and I mirror him.

'It suits you – this body, I mean.'

He holds up a hand as if analysing it, trying to find a secret within his palm. 'I do feel stronger.' He turns towards the fire once more, and I find myself wanting his attention again.

'Why are you so quiet? Are you hungry? Do you need me to find someone for you to feed on?'

He stiffens but says nothing.

'If you don't tell me what's wrong, I can't help you.'

Silence envelops us a moment before he speaks, so quietly I find myself leaning in to hear better.

'Why did you lie to me?'

My brow rises at his accusation. 'I've always spoken the truth to you.'

'No, you haven't. You claimed to love me.'

My body jerks in shock. The moment I first laid eyes on him, I wanted him – wanted to protect him and keep him safe from my kind and their escapades in the city. Why would he think I *didn't* love him?

'My love for you has always been obvious. The turn has probably made you feel vulnerable, my love. Let us eat, and you'll feel much more like yourself.'

He reluctantly glances my way and lifts a hand to stroke my cheek, trailing his fingers through my hair. The touch brings me warmth, and I lean into his fingers.

I could experience this love for the rest of my immortal life.

The thought widens my smile.

'What are you thinking about?' he asks.

'How I'll never get bored of us, bored of this,' I say, motioning between us.

Slowly he lifts my chin, our faces so close together my eyes lower to his lips, wanting nothing more than to taste him. My hands roam up and down his body, feeling his new-found strength, and I feel my desire growing with his proximity.

'You're so much stronger,' I murmur.

'I am stronger,' he states, pinning me against his chest so our bodies are joined. His usual human warmth is gone, but in its place is a force I find myself magnetised by.

I raise my arms and wrap my hands around his neck, feeling the puncture wounds on both sides. I frown and peer up, finding his stone-cold face.

'I am dangerous,' he adds.

The words make my heart race. He and I will be

43

formidable. We will have each other's back for eternity. Excitement lances through my limbs, making my fingers tingle as I run them over his cold skin, into his dark hair.

'I am a *monster*,' he whispers.

I stiffen. 'What—'

He grips my throat tightly, causing my words to come to a forced stop.

'You will let me talk. You will listen, and you will not move until I say so,' he commands, his words pushing against my will. His persuasion is stronger than my ability to block it. For once in my life, he has power over me. Before now, he could never hurt me. 'You betrayed me, Victoria. You asked your father to turn me against my wishes. I thought you *loved* me.'

'I do love you!' I choke out, but his grasp doesn't waver.

'No. You love yourself.'

My attempt to loosen his grip is futile. My body is no longer under my command. His hands are immovable, and for once, I feel small and weak in comparison – his power over me is unyielding.

'You took everything away from me – my life, my dreams, my cousin – all because you wanted me for *yourself*. That, Victoria, is not called love. It's called *selfishness*.'

His fingers press in dangerously tight, and my lungs begin to burn. I merely look up at him, meeting his hateful gaze.

'I made the choice you were too scared to make,' I whisper, knowing this to be true. I could see his curiosity from a mile away, but he was too frightened to take the risk.

'Yes, and now, in return, I'll choose *your* fate. I'll make a life-altering decision for *you*,' he says, his grip on me loosening.

I try to bolt, but his persuasion still holds me hostage.

He leans down to caress my cheek with his own. 'I'll deal with you the same way I dealt with your coven – with your father.'

My eyes dart towards the fire before us. I asked how he had got the fire blazing. It seems I've got my answer.

'Yes, Victoria,' he confirms, making my eyes close briefly. 'Your father and brethren are all dead. They were too weak to fight me, their powers no match for a youngling.'

'I don't believe you,' I murmur. 'My Dimitri would never hurt anyone.'

'Your Dimitri died the moment his cousin was murdered in cold blood. Your Dimitri died the moment he told his family to run away from him and never look back. *Your* Dimitri died the moment you decided he wasn't enough for you as a human.'

Our eyes clash, and I can finally see all his emotions on display. Every bit of hurt, grief, suffering and loss is in them. My heart shatters seeing him – all of him.

'I'm sorry.'

His hands are nimble as they smoothly wrap around my neck, a hand either side of my head in an affectionate hold. My own hands twitch, wanting to find his wrists and hold on to them like anchors.

'I am a monster,' he repeats quietly.

'Please don't do this. This isn't you,' I whimper.

Eyes full of cold, calm hatred stare back at me. He's right. My Dimitri is gone. Before me isn't the man I loved but a demon waiting to unleash itself.

'Goodbye, Victoria.'

Too quickly for me to register, he grabs my skull in between his hands more firmly and roughly twists with extraordinary vampire force, snapping my neck with a definitive crack.

EPILOGUE

150 Years Later

The bottle of Liquid Gold hangs precariously from my fingers, my eyes half-open as I stumble through the street. Passers-by keep their distance but don't baulk any more. They have become accustomed to me, the only vampire in the city now.

I am alone. *Always* alone.

My foot catches on something, and I go flying, too weak to save myself from face-planting on the street. I hear something smash, and I groan. The glass bottle is no longer full but now leaking over the ground I lie upon, dribbling slowly as I watch it with contempt.

'Fuck you,' I mutter.

'Are you talking to the drink?' someone asks.

My head turns, and I note two black leather boots. They are scuffed, and I'm certain I can see a sliver of toe through one of them. The hole is not quite big enough to be noticeable to a human, but to me, it's plainly obvious.

Further up I find a pair of small, gangly legs – both with patches on them, different-coloured materials stitched over the brown trousers they wear. The stranger's top seems like the only part of their attire that is somewhat decent, until the stain at the neck comes into view. My effort to see more is now making me roll onto my back.

Dark crimson eyes stare down at me with curiosity. My heart hammers, thinking I've missed a vampire in my life's mission to rid Rubien of them all, but I realise that is not what this child is – not quite, anyway. The young girl's hair is long and dark red, tied up with a piece of leather. Her arms are covered with cuts and bruises, and some of her fingers are bent at strange angles.

'Are you all right? Do you need help?' she asks, seeming to understand I'm not capable of answering her last question. 'You're a vampire, right? Is this what happens when you don't feed? You get weak and start crawling around the city? Do you need me to fetch you some blood?'

Blood.

My stomach clenches at the word. My mouth salivates over it. I want it so bad, but no. That's not the plan. The plan is to fade away and never open my eyes again. I've made it this far, and I can't stop now. I've failed too many times before – but not this time.

Sixty-seven days and counting.

'No. Leave me alone,' I mutter, my throat dry as sand.

She studies me, injured hands entwining, and winces at her movements. I see a large silver scar on her right palm. She notes my stare and holds it up.

'I would have left you alone, but it claims I'm safe.'

I have no idea what she's talking about, but my stare never wavers from her. The child's interest in me is somewhat beguiling. I've not spoken to another person in a *very* long time who hasn't looked at me with disgust, suspicion or fear.

'What are you doing here?' I ask.

'I escaped.'

'From whom?'

'The Ravens.'

'Ravens?' I utter, realising too slowly what she is. A Raven. Of course. Half vampire, half dameer. The magical race that lives within the deeper parts of the cave. 'How did you get to this side of the wall?' I ask.

'There's a hole.'

I tilt my head, knowing from experience there is no hole in the wall between the city of Rubien and the House of Raven. We've been separated for as long as I can remember – unless they've built something recently.

'Lies. There is no hole,' I reply.

The girl's smirk is full of amusement. She seems like the quietly confident type. What surprises me more, though, is her fear is non-existent. I can't scent anything on her which confirms her vampire ancestry.

'There is now.' She shrugs. 'But I've heard the royal family wants to make a proper tunnel. It's a pain for them to travel to us.'

'Is that so?'

She nods. 'Yes. I overheard our leader say so. She didn't sound too pleased about it.'

The view from where I lie nauseates me. I need to get up. So I roll to my side and attempt to get to my feet. In seconds she's clutching my arm to aid me as I stagger to a standing position. My hand is still holding the broken bottle of liquor. I pause and study her, wondering why she is assisting me and not fleeing.

'What? Do you not like touch?' she asks, her youthful face rippling with understanding.

The recognition in her features pains me. It's as if she knows exactly what it's like to hate people touching her. I ponder over what she has endured within her House – her arms are an obvious display of what she's experienced, marks coating her pale skin, alongside dark scabs and slowly healing wounds.

'What happened there?' I ask, pointing to a long gash across her forearm. It looks to have been stitched by a very inexperienced hand. I conclude she's done it herself – her handiwork is dismal.

'Master Jye sliced me open.' She hesitates before continuing. 'He asked me to perform a job, and I wasn't fast enough for his liking. It's all right, though. I'm used to it.' She smiles as if to calm *me*, to make *me* feel better.

My frown deepens. 'That's torture,' I state.

A scowl forms on her small face as I stand to my full form, looming over her. A predator and its prey. I can't help but feel awfully dangerous around her, like any moment I'll snap. I'll feed off her, and I'll be back to my normal state, and I'll be alone all over again. I don't dare move, knowing that with the thoughts in my head, I'm a threat to her. I need her to leave. To leave me be and go on her way. Or else she'll be the next dinner I planned on never having.

'Torture?' She scrunches her nose up. 'The Elder Raven calls it discipline.'

My snort is unexpected, surprising us both. 'No. Discipline does not involve hurting someone, especially when it's dealt out with weapons.'

She doesn't say anything but takes a step away from me, probably assuming I'm fine now I'm standing. 'Do you need some blood? I can see if the butcher has some spare.'

The offer is unexpected, but I shake my head. 'No. I have a plan that I can't get out of.'

'Which is?'

'To die of starvation.'

The girl cocks her head. 'How long have you been without blood?'

'Sixty-seven days.'

'No wonder you look so terrible. I heard vampires are supposed to have everlasting beauty.'

My unimpressed face makes her grin.

'Why starvation?' she asks.

'I killed all those who wronged me – wronged this city,' I admit, but she doesn't react. If anything, she probably understands more than anyone else – her House is notorious for being radical and unethical. 'And now I'm alone. But I'm too much of a coward to kill myself. I'm hoping if I weaken myself enough, someone will find me and finish the job.'

Dark crimson eyes widen only slightly. I've frightened her. Not with what I am but with my wish to end my life.

'Life is hard,' she mutters with a shrug. 'And some days are unbearable, but do you want to know what I tell myself when I feel like giving up?'

I refrain from sighing but shrug in response. 'What?'

'It's going to be hard, but *hard* does not mean *impossible*. You'll be all right. Things will work out in the end.'

The words clang through my skull, sending shivers down my arms. My eyes swivel towards her, studying her, taking her in. My mother said something similar once. She, too, was a person full of optimism. Memories of her flood my thoughts, something I've not allowed since her death.

'You've paled. I didn't think that was possible for someone who is already so fair.'

My eyes snap to the girl who pulls me out of my thoughts. She's so small, so fragile and so naive. She thinks that being tortured daily is a temporary situation, like each day is a step closer to seeing the sun, to finding a sliver of happiness.

My silence seems to spur her to fill in the gap. 'What is your name, vampire?'

'Dimitri Thunders,' I say after a moment, finding her dark crimson eyes looking up at me. They remind me of red wine – dark and mysterious, intelligent in more ways than one.

She wears a faint smile upon her face, her tiny fangs more adorable than intimidating. Somehow she seems to know she's had an effect on me. She sticks out her small hand, the one with the scar, a few of her recently broken fingers looking disturbingly mangled. The sight enrages me as I carefully grasp her small hand in mine, taking care not to squeeze too hard.

'Nice to meet you, Dimitri Thunders.' Her smile is genuine, and it creates a flicker of something inside my chest. I've not felt anything for so long. I have not felt the feeling of *hope* in so long.

How has this malnourished child slithered her way through my shields so easily?

Because you are desperate for companionship, and she is the first one to see you as a person and not the true monster you are, a voice says inside my head.

Ignoring my thoughts, I say, 'What is *your* name?'

She rolls her shoulders, looking around as if any moment someone will come for her. A small part of me wishes to protect her, to shield the girl from whoever is causing her harm.

'My name is Scarlet Seraphine.'

Author Note

Hi there!

I hope you enjoyed reading COVEN OF VAMPIRES.

Thank you so much for purchasing this book and for taking the time to get to know Dimitri. Please consider leaving a review or recommending it to a friend.

Hannah x

ACKNOWLEDGMENTS

First I'd like to thank my beta readers — Teresa and Amber. You guys give the best advice and ideas. I'm grateful and so lucky to be able to work with you both and hope we can work together again in the future. Thank you!

Second I'd like to thank those who have read my debut novel **The Crimson Scar** and messaged saying how much you loved Dimitri. He's been a favourite of mine from the very beginning and making his origin story felt like the natural next step. I thought he deserved a little something extra and this little snippet of his past is one I hope you enjoy. For those that have asked if Dimitri will be coming back at any stage…. I have plans for him in the future! So stay tuned, our vampire baby will make another appearance.

And lastly I want to thank my family for their support — you know who you are. You're the best and I love you all dearly!

About the Author

Hannah is a Slytherin, Gemini, and a lover of all things fantasy and chocolate. When she isn't writing you can find her curled up with a cup of a tea and a good book. When she *is* writing you can find her googling synonyms and scrolling Pinterest for inspiration.

Hannah published her debut THE CRIMSON SCAR, hoping to bring the stories stuck in her head to life. Now she is self publishing COVEN OF VAMPIRES in the hopes others will enjoy diving back into her fantasy world.

Want to know more?
Visit: www.hannahpenfoldauthor.com
Socials: hannahpenfoldauthor

ALSO BY HANNAH...

THE CRIMSON SCAR

Scarlet Seraphine should never have been born. Living in the House of Raven - the home of a race with magic and vampire blood - she is an outcast and wants nothing more than to escape her life of confinement.

But everything changes with the announcement of the Hex Trials - a deadly competition in which Ravens lose their lives at every turn. Scarlet is forced to abandon her plans to leave for a chance to claim one of the trials' most valuable prizes, the only medicine that can save her sister's life.

With time running out and her sister's fate hanging in the balance, Scarlet has no choice but to compete. Death follows closely in every trial, and with a target on her back, Scarlet must decide whether fighting for her sister's life is worth losing her own.

TURN THE PAGE FOR THE FIRST FEW CHAPTERS...

1

I breathe in the smell of sweat as spectators roar at me, their shouts loud and invasive from outside the fighting ring. All I need to focus on, though, is the man in front of me. He's perhaps a few years older than me – early twenties. He has a mop of dark, messy hair upon his head, and from the way he smells, I can tell he is dameer – a human born with magic.

Spit flies from his mouth as he attempts to dodge my attacks. Occasionally I let his fists collide with my bare skin to keep the fight interesting, to let him think he has a chance. I glance quickly at the manager of the joint. Storm, a burly man with pure white eyes, gives me a nod of permission.

You can finish the fight now, he conveys silently, and I grin wickedly.

My first fight, I was told off for ending it in less than thirty seconds, Storm scolding me for not performing to his liking. 'Make them beg for a victory,' he'd said.

If I triumphed within seconds, it wouldn't be as entertaining for his customers, and the more they are entertained, the more money they throw his way.

My opponent swings for my gut. I'm quick to elude the attack. My own fist flies towards his jaw in answer, the crack loud in my ears. *Bingo.* In one smooth movement, my opponent's body falls to the floor, his eyes rolling back into his head.

'And the winner is the Phoenix!' Storm cries out, sending the crowd of spectators into a roar of equal amounts of delight that I've won and horror that I've lost them money.

One voice I hear above the others is the vampire who is a regular here and who just so happens to be my best friend. Dimitri Thunders' cheers of happiness are loud compared to everyone else's. I turn towards Dimitri, who grins widely, and I mirror him in high spirits.

'Nicely done,' he says with a nod as I approach the small wall that divides the fighters from the spectators. We clap hands as we usually do after every win, my fingerless gloves damp with sweat and blood.

'Thank you,' I whisper with a grin.

I reach under my hood and wipe at my eyes. The mask makes it difficult, but I'm used to it. A rule here at the Badger's Sett is no fighter is allowed to show their identity, and thus, fighters are made to wear hooded costumes and masks to cover the face – eyes not included.

Workers drag my opponent away for the next fight to commence. Storm announces who the next fighters will be and urges everyone to get their bet and beer ready for the next round.

I jump over the small wall and follow Dimitri to the bar. Some men slap me on the shoulder in congratulations, while others scowl at me.

At the bar, a young man called Andre is serving. When he sees me in my fighting gear, he starts moving. Two glasses of Liquid Gold are ready on the counter when I reach him.

'There you go, love.'

I nod my head in silent thanks. I smile under my mask, knowing he won't be able to see it, but I still see a twinkle in his eyes, a common reaction for humans to have in the presence of the Phoenix.

The next match is about to begin, so Dimitri and I head upstairs. We walk past private rooms all designated for the fighters to unwind and safely unravel their hidden identities. Dimitri heads for the end chamber, my preferred space, called the Green Room.

The walls and furniture are all an emerald green, and it has a minibar within that Dimitri and I take full advantage of. It's also a safe place for me to take off my hood and sweaty mask.

'That was fun,' I state happily, adrenaline still coursing through me as I untie my long dark red hair, the tension instantly soothed the moment my locks spring free of their plait.

'You kept your guard up well, Scar. He didn't have a chance,' Dimitri says loyally as his glamour drops.

While in my fighting form, known as the Phoenix, Dimitri holds the glamour of an older gentleman, a father figure watching his child win fights. The first time I saw his disguise, I thought it was hilarious, his belly slightly rotund and his beard long and highlighted with grey.

But when I am simply Scarlet, he is the complete opposite of a simple human man. Dimitri without magic is a tall, dark-haired vampire with fangs longer than mine and a smile just as deadly.

I take a long swig of Liquid Gold from my glass, letting the alcohol soothe me. As the name suggests, the drink is pure gold in colour and stains a person's mouth metallic, but I don't care – I've earned it.

Gold liquor dribbles from the side of my mouth as I drain my glass, and my tongue pokes out to catch it before it trickles down my chin.

'Good?' Dimitri asks, taking a swig of his own.

Liquid Gold is a special beverage that tastes like the individual's preferred flavour. A drop of magic makes it delicious to anyone over eighteen and vile to anyone underage.

'Like chocolate and mint,' I tell him, rubbing my belly to show how tasty it is.

'Like strawberries and cream,' he counters, rubbing his own stomach.

A warm sensation courses through me as I relish the alcohol before shouts from the balcony echo through the room. We both head to the terrace, a pane of one-way glass protecting us from eyes below, and see two men. One is new, from the looks of him, while also young and toned. The other is a crowd favourite. They call him the Pirate, as he has a wooden leg and massive arms that can easily crush a man's skull. I've yet to fight him, but I'm not eager to.

'Put your bets in,' Storm shouts from the ring, hands up in the air to get the audience's attention. 'We have the Pirate and the Teacher.'

I share a look with my friend. 'The Teacher? What type of name is that?' I scoff.

There aren't many names that sound good here in the Badger's Sett. I chose the Phoenix because I thought it sounded distinctive and intimidating, but the Teacher? It doesn't even *sound* menacing.

'Maybe he wants to be a professor when he's older,' Dimitri ponders.

I shrug, not bothering to watch the fight – I know the Teacher will probably be beaten within minutes. I head back to the Green Room to change into my normal clothes, my belongings waiting in a trunk.

I'm stuffing my sweaty clothes into my sack when I hear Dimitri shouting. Rushing out to the balcony, I find a look of astonishment upon his pale face.

'What happened?' I ask.

'The Teacher.' He points to the fight below. The Pirate, on his backside, looks up into the eyes of the young masked man. 'He trounced the Pirate. Flipped him like a pancake!'

The Teacher's body language shows he isn't threatened. He seems to know he has won, and the crowd screams around him as he puts his boot upon the Pirate's stomach in warning.

As if knowing he is being watched, the man looks up at us. I don't baulk but rather tilt my head questioningly.

Who is this new fighter?

The Teacher stares in our direction for a moment more, light blue eyes stony. Then he salutes as if sensing us still watching him.

'Cocky bastard.' Dimitri laughs, clapping his hands for the fighter as he returns to his opponent and helps him up onto his feet. 'What a show. You missed a good one there, Scar.'

'Yeah, shame I missed it,' I answer half-heartedly, curious as to how someone of the Teacher's size could defeat a half giant like the Pirate.

Dimitri and I stay most of the night at the Badger's Sett, watching fights and downing Liquid Gold. Unfortunately, being part vampire, I can't get drunk on alcohol, and neither can Dimitri, but we still enjoy swindling newcomers with drinking games.

The evening is quiet when we leave, most households in bed, already sleeping as we stroll leisurely through the streets. The cavern above us is pitch black and menacing, the cave much colder now than it is during the day.

The homes here are painted bright colours, their front porches decorated with potted plants and creative welcome mats. Here in the city of Rubien, the humans and dameer live happily together.

'Sometimes I wish I were human,' I murmur, fingering my belt of daggers.

Dimitri nods in understanding. His human life was taken from him too soon, and for hundreds of years, he's been living the life of a blood drinker. He would never complain to me about it, but I know he hates his food choices.

'It's hard,' he agrees, his hands finding his pockets. 'But I can't complain to *you*, of all people. I'm accepted for who I am here.' He waves to the city around us.

It's true – the people of Rubien accept Dimitri, sympathising with his past. It isn't uncommon for humans and dameer to be caught in the wrong place at the wrong time. Vampires can be dangerous and scary creatures – at least the foul ones – and when caught, it is near impossible to run away from them.

'They are coming to accept me. It's slow, but I've noticed a change over the years,' I reply, knowing deep down the people of Rubien would have embraced me sooner if it weren't for my Raven heritage.

We approach the wall that divides the city of Rubien and the House of Raven. It's an intimidatingly tall stack of jagged rocks that was created as a barrier to keep the humans out. Or as the humans claim, to keep us Ravens out.

We walk along the barricade, sharp stone edges poking out, before we reach a tunnel. The temperature here increases a few degrees. As the only entrance to my home, it's the only way I can travel to see Dimitri.

He stops suddenly, his hand shooting out to grasp my shoulder. I'm suddenly on high alert, my hands out in case he faints, in case he stumbles. It wouldn't be the first time that's happened.

'Dimitri?' My senses sharpen at the seriousness of his expression as he comes back from wherever he just went.

'I had a strange feeling.' Dimitri's gaze wanders to the tunnel, the same tunnel I've been travelling through for years now, as if it's dangerous. His bright red eyes dart around the opening, surveying the space.

Peering down the entrance myself, I find nothing out of the ordinary. 'My hand isn't bleeding,' I say, checking my hand for any blood.

My right hand, scarred with a jagged silver line, peers up at me. From birth I've had it, and from birth it has been able to sense when danger is coming. When I came across a stray dog once, my scar opened up, pouring out crimson – the dog nearly bit my hand clean off right after. But right now, the scar is silver in colour and sealed shut. I know I'm safe. For now.

Dimitri grimaces, his brow creasing with thought. It's not uncommon for him to have these strange feelings. When he was a dameer, a human born with magic, he could see the future. However, now, as a vampire, the only inkling of his ability comes in the form of various strong feelings and blurry visions.

'I think it's safe for you to get home,' he declares.

I wait a beat to see if he will explain himself, but he doesn't. He simply waves me down the tunnel instead. The hole in the wall is the furthest he will go.

I slowly make my way through, and when I get to the end, I take a cautious look around. Again nothing seems out of the norm.

'I'll be fine,' I tell Dimitri, meeting his watchful gaze across the way, waving my scarred hand at him. 'Nothing happening here.'

He doesn't look convinced, but he nods. 'Okay. Go straight home. No shortcuts.'

'Yes, sir.' I salute, making his lips twitch with amusement.

2

It's quiet in the House of Raven, much like the city of Rubien, but that's where the similarities stop. Here, the houses aren't colourfully painted like those of the humans over the wall. Instead, they are cold and neutral in colour and blend in with the cold cave interior. None of the Ravens have bothered to decorate their homes – no plants or personal belongings to set each place apart from the others.

I follow one of the lava rivers that flow through the depths of the cavern. It bubbles beside me, reminding me how painful it will be if I topple into it. I take a few steps away to be safe.

The stream leads me to the end of my street, where homes are packed together in close proximity. In this part of the cave, the stalactites dangle intimidatingly above me, the cavern ceiling we all live under a dark, gaping hole where bats and other nocturnal creatures sleep.

After passing a number of small stone homes, I come to my own household. I can see from the gap underneath the front door that a light is on. *Who is up at this time of night?* Stepping through the entrance, I'm welcomed by my older sister Roux at the dinner table, her face cautious until she registers it's me.

'Hey.' She smiles, in the middle of cutting off the skin of an apple.

'Hey there. Cravings?' I ask, watching her eat the juicy red skin of her fruit. She nods, and my eyes fall to her swelling belly. 'How are they doing?'

Roux's hand automatically goes to her pregnant stomach, rubbing it affectionately before answering. 'I had another check-up today.'

I sit at the table alongside her. I don't particularly like to talk about her check-ups – the House of Raven is well known for its clinical way of reproducing.

Roux is classed as a breeder; her duty is to procreate. She's to keep breeding as many Ravens as possible so that our House will thrive for generations to come. Being female, she is allowed to stay home, but my older brother Ash isn't so lucky. He is forced to lodge with other males in a shared residence near the breeding clinic, forbidden to have visitors.

'And? How did the check-up go?' I probe, noting Roux's downcast gaze, the apple in her hand temporarily forgotten. Suddenly her eyes become teary, and I'm reaching for her, not sure why she is upset. 'Roux, what happened? Is something wrong with the babies?'

Roux stares up at the ceiling, trying her best not to blink. I know this is a way of preventing herself from crying, as I do the same when I'm trying to hold myself together.

'The healers don't think they'll make it through the birth,' Roux admits in a whisper.

My shoulders sag at the news. 'What? *Why?* Why do they say that?'

'Purely because they're twins.'

I shake my head in frustration. 'Yes, but Ember and Blaze are proof twins can be birthed without complications,' I argue, mentioning our other siblings. 'What makes *your* babies any different?'

'Me,' Roux states coldly, her voice turning hard like she truly believes she's the problem. 'I can't birth them without some sort of help. They don't think *I'll* make it through the birth, let alone stay alive long enough for the babies to survive.'

Fear instantly wells up inside my chest. Heartbreaking images of Roux and the babies fog my mind. Desperation claws at me. I can't lose my sister. I can't lose my future family. Not like this.

'What type of help are we talking about? What can help you, Roux?' I demand, my voice loud enough that she hushes me and looks with worry at the staircase that leads upstairs to where our mother sleeps.

'It's taken Ruby hours to get to sleep,' Roux explains, pressing a finger to her lips.

When I nod in confirmation that I won't start shouting again she continues.

'They mentioned a certain medicine I can take leading up to the birth, but it's very hard to come by, and as you can imagine, it's in high demand.'

My mouth twists in frustration. I remember Ruby mentioning taking special medicine when she was in labour with my brother and sister. What did she take, and how did she acquire it?

'Well, that's utter horse shit,' I mutter before silence envelops us both. I meet her gaze, and we both watch each other as tears fall from our eyes. A tear each for a future we can't prevent.

'Other than that, the babies are happy and healthy.' Roux wipes at her face, already looking guilty for putting me in a dark mood. She takes my hand and squeezes it, as if *I'm* the one who needs the comfort right now.

'Roux,' I say, but I have no idea what to say. Roux is in

danger. Her children are at risk. Surely there is something I can do. 'I'll find the medicine for you. We have time.'

'That's sweet of you, Scar, but if the healers can't obtain it for me, I doubt you'll be able to.'

I think of the money I've won from my fights, the velvet bags I've accumulated over the years, which I keep stored at Dimitri's place. 'It doesn't matter how much it costs. I'll get the medicine for you. I don't care what I have to do. You and the babies will pull through.'

'You don't—' Roux begins, but I cut her off, my feelings tumultuous at this point.

'No, Roux. I don't care how I acquire it. I'm going to save you all. Raven's promise.'

Always the intelligent sister out of us, she doesn't bother arguing. She knows once I set my mind on something, I'll work hard to prove I can do it, and with this, I promise myself I won't give up until I find a way for Roux to watch her children grow up.

3

'You're looking for Araside, love. Very powerful stuff,' the woman tells me.

I'm up early the next day, walking the markets of Rubien and asking anyone and everyone I can about this mysterious medicine that can help pregnant women deliver babies. The very few people who do know what I'm talking about confirm my suspicions that the substance is expensive and very rare.

'So I won't be able to find Araside without leaving this cave?' I ask.

The woman shakes her head with a sympathetic grimace. 'No, love. The last I heard of it, it was found near the forests of the kingdom of Envy, which without a portal would be at least a few months' travel on horse,' she answers, looking at the metal bracelet around my wrist, the one all Ravens wear – a bracelet that prevents us from leaving this cave.

I grimace, wanting nothing more than to scream and shout with frustration. 'Thanks for your time.'

After hours of zero luck, I decide to head back to the House of Raven, defeated and angry. Somehow I have to find a way to retrieve a substance that comes from a kingdom I can't get to. What has my life become?

'Hello, Gem,' I say as I walk into work, entering the large double doors of a stone-walled barn full of horses. In a cave, wood is a hard material to come by, so everything is mainly made of rock or metal. The whole place lacks a homely feel, and I hate it.

I pet Gem on her soft nose and give her neck a scratch. 'What am I going to do?' I whisper to her, my mind reeling with questions. Gem softly grazes my clothes, looking for a treat I don't have. 'Okay, okay. I'll get you something to eat.' I chuckle half-heartedly while turning for the tack room.

I stop in my tracks, sensing something not quite right. The horses don't seem to feel threatened, their heads poking out of their stalls like usual when I arrive. I sniff the air – no scent other than the animals, but that means nothing. All of us that possess vampire blood are born without a smell.

Silently I peer over Gem's stall, taking a look inside to see if there is someone there. There isn't. I move to the next stall, where a mare called Torment lives, but again no one is there. I repeat this for all the horses until only the tack room is left.

I reach for a broom that leans against a nearby wall before I twist the handle on the door. The moment I open it, I can't help but smile.

Sitting on a bucket, wearing his fighting leathers, is my older brother Blaze. He is cleaning his boots with some oil when he looks up at me, his curly red hair bouncing when he moves.

'What are you doing here?' I say in greeting, watching him finish off his boots. They look pretty good after a polish.

'I thought I'd stop by and say hello, but you weren't here. So I thought I'd spend my time doing something useful while I waited.' He shrugs, crimson eyes gleaming with amusement.

He starts to put the polish and brush away, stashing them in the wrong places. I roll my eyes and move them to their correct spots, earning a fanged grin from my brother, his teeth inhumanly white. He takes the broom off me and twirls it around, expertly spinning it around his body with ease.

'You've been out a lot lately. Is everything okay?' he asks, walking through a routine of strikes and defence movements.

I shrug because I don't know how to answer. Lately I've been fighting a lot at the Badger's Sett, which Blaze and the rest of my family don't know about.

I watch with mild interest as he continues his fight with an imaginary opponent, his body supple as it attacks and counter-attacks his invisible foe.

'Yeah, I'm all right. Just doing stuff.' I shrug again when he looks my way.

'Doing stuff?' he echoes, pausing for a brief moment.

'Yeah. I've been working hard to get some extra money.'

He seems to defeat his unseeable opponent and decides to call it a day, placing the broom against the wall. 'Why do you want extra money? Is there something you're saving up for?'

My freedom, I think sourly. If I had enough money, I could pay a blacksmith to take this awful bracelet off my wrist, and I could run to another city. I could run away and let my family live without the embarrassment of me lingering in their lives.

Instead, I say, 'New boots.'

Blaze surveys my tatty old brown boots and scowls. 'Your masters don't give you new ones every year?'

I give him an irritated look. Like Roux, my brother has a duty, but it's to fight. As a fighter, he trains for the occasion when we may go to war, or for when the royal family needs him for a more specific mission.

'If they do, they've forgotten to swing by for the last three years,' I state.

I'm not classed as a fighter; I'm classed as a worker. Someone who's given one job to do for the rest of their life.

In my case, I tend to the horses and get paid very little money for it.

A sudden sensation in my right hand makes me gasp in surprise. Blaze surveys my scarred palm with a scowl, the jagged mark seeping crimson blood as if it's a fresh wound. Right now my blood is a red flag warning me something is coming.

I hurry to the entrance of the stables, where I find Master Jepp pouring buckets of water from each of the stalls onto the floor. I refrain from shouting rude remarks at him.

'What is the meaning of this?' the older male asks, his black uniform with red detailing sleek and intimidating as he prowls closer. 'You give these wretched animals dirty water?'

He runs a hand through his bright red hair, the same colour as Blaze's, the same shade as every Raven's – except mine.

'I fill their buckets up with fresh water every morning,' I answer matter-of-factly, willing my face into neutrality. I keep my hands behind my back to hide the bleeding and to stop myself from wrapping them around his stupid neck.

'What are we paying you for around here?' Master Jepp snaps.

You barely pay me at all, I want to answer, but I don't, knowing if I play along with his little game, I'll be sent to the leader of our House for punishment, and that's the last thing I want.

Master Jepp slowly approaches me, looking me up and down with distaste. 'You never did have a backbone, half-blood,' he mutters, circling me like an animal would its prey.

I stand very still, willing myself to breathe as slowly as possible, to focus on that instead of his words.

'If I were Ruby, I would have given you away to the humans and never looked back.'

An aching pain in my mouth informs me of my rising anger. My fangs grow slowly as frustration begins to swell inside my chest. As a child, I would have slapped him by now, but I learned early on that people like him thrive on power, and if I played the victim, he would indulge in my squirming.

Master Jepp's smile falls further the longer I stay quiet, ignoring his jibes. 'Do your job properly *half-blood*,' he spits, sensing my need to bite back slowly fade away. 'Or else *she'll* hear about this.'

Finally breaking eye contact, the master notices Blaze behind me. His features quickly morph into a rare smile as he forgets me instantly. 'Good to see you, Blaze. How's your twin?'

'Ember is very well,' Blaze says politely.

'How is Ember's combat training coming along? Still top of the class?'

Blaze's mouth twitches at the dig, but he stays composed. 'Excelling as usual, Master.'

'Marvellous. I look forward to her joining my classes. I've heard she is a remarkable student.' Master Jepp nods pleasantly before turning on his heel and leaving us without another word.

I turn to Blaze with a scowl, hatred still simmering in my bones. 'Holy Hanrah! How does anyone cope with him? He is the bane of my existence.'

Blaze shakes his head. 'He's not that bad, really. He's actually a really good teacher to have. It's only you he's a jerk to.'

'Good to know,' I utter, looking at the buckets of water that need refilling. 'I swear he only visits me to make my life harder.'

Blaze leans against a stall, the horse closest to him curious enough to sniff him. Blaze eyes the stallion up before meeting my gaze. 'Ruby would never give you away,' he blurts, making me blink with surprise. 'She's never regretted having you, Scar.'

Discomfort weaves its way through me. It's strange to have Blaze feel sympathy for me, or for him to feel sorry enough for me to think I need reassurance that our mother loves me.

'I know that.' I shrug.

Ruby, our mother, was once as loved and adored in the House of Raven as our sister Ember is now. She grew up as one of the youngest breeders and had four children. Then, having surpassed her duty at an early age, she was invited to become a fighter and join the Raven army, but that all changed when she had me.

She would never admit it, but I know Ruby misses her old life, training like Blaze and Ember do every day. Now she serves as a barkeeper at the local tavern and works long hours to keep us fed and watered. Not once, though, have I heard her complain about her job, and she has never made me feel any less than my siblings for being a worker too – even though it's seen as lower class in our House.

'Master Jepp only says things like that to aggravate me. He'll find any excuse to send me off for punishment,' I clarify, finding a rag and wiping the blood from my hand. Now that Master Jepp has left, the once-crimson scar is now a silver stripe upon my palm.

Blaze nods, crossing his arms. Silence envelops us for a moment before I approach him.

'So what's the real reason for your visit? Gossip on any new trainees? Or have you been missing me?'

My brother's face widens into an amused smile, bright red eyes looking down at me. 'The last one, I think, is stretching it a bit.'

'You'd be surprised how many visits I get in a day from people needing to see this beautiful face,' I counter with a wide smile.

He grins, but it doesn't reach his eyes. I know then that his visit has something to do with what I've been thinking about since last night.

'I'm worried about Roux,' he admits, lowering his voice.

'She's pretending everything is okay, but I heard her cry today when she thought she was home alone. It can't be good for the kids.'

I grimace, feeling the pressure rise inside me. Time – I just need time to think of a solution.

'I've been asking around the city,' I say, gaining Blaze's attention. Unlike me, he never visits the city of Rubien, having been brought up to think humans are below him and thus not worth his time.

'And?' he prompts, leaning forward slightly, anticipating my next words.

'I'm told the medicine Roux needs is called Araside, but it's found in the kingdom of Envy.'

'Envy!' Blaze blurts with horror. 'How the hell are we supposed to get there?'

I shrug. 'We need a portal. We need a witch or a wizard to take us there.'

Blaze lifts up his arm, putting the metal bracelet on his wrist up to my face. 'And how are we supposed to deal with these?'

My eyes roam over the band. It's said that once a Raven leaves the cave, the bracelet will begin to burn them, a precaution for Ravens who feel the need to leave their House and desert their loyalties. Personally, I think it says more about the leadership than us.

'It will hurt like hell,' I state without hesitation, and Blaze reluctantly nods.

Our conversation is interrupted by a sound I've not heard in years. A bell.

It chimes, echoing through the stables. The horses go crazy in answer. I mirror Blaze's frown when I meet his gaze.

'The Elder Raven? What does she want?' Blaze wonders.

'This better be good,' I huff, hurrying to lock up the barn before making my way to the Raven's Nest.

WANT MORE OF
THE CRIMSON SCAR?

Scan to buy your next favourite read!

Printed in Great Britain
by Amazon